Nos Gust...

We...

Brooklin
Braliynn

Nos Gusta Comer Bien
We Like to Eat Well

Bi-Lingual Edition

ELYSE APRIL

Ilustrado por Lewis Agrell

Series de Salud para la Familia / Family Health Series

HOHM PRESS
Prescott, Arizona

Diseño de la portada:The Agrell Group:www.theagrellgroup.com
Diseño del libro: The Agrell Group, lagrell@commspeed.net

Library of Congress Cataloging-in-Publication Data

April, Elyse.
[We like to eat well. Spanish & English]
Nos gusta comer bien = We like to eat well / Elyse April ; ilustrado por Lewis Agrell. -- Bilingual ed.
    p. cm. -- (We like to)
Parallel text in English and Spanish; translated from the English.
ISBN 978-1-890772-96-3 (trade paper : alk. paper)
1. Nutrition--Juvenile literature. 2. Health--Juvenile literature. I. Agrell, Lewis. II. Title. III. Title: Nos gusta comer bien.
RA784.A665182 2009
613.2--dc22
                        2009016091

HOHM PRESS
P.O. Box 2501
Prescott, AZ 86302
800-381-2700

www.hohmpress.com

Este libro fue impreso en China.

Ilustración de la portada: Lewis Agrell • Traducido por Jocelyn DelRio

Para Paul

For Paul

Lo fresco y lo verde.

We like to eat fresh.

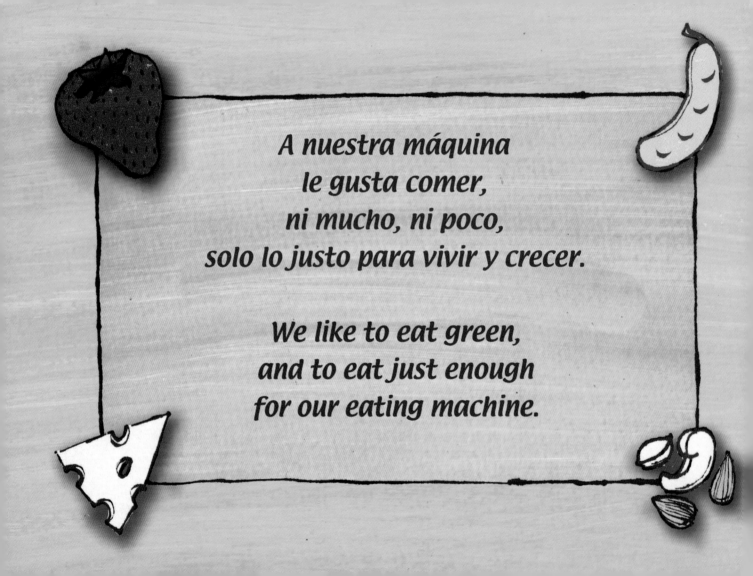

A nuestra máquina
le gusta comer,
ni mucho, ni poco,
solo lo justo para vivir y crecer.

We like to eat green,
and to eat just enough
for our eating machine.

Lo blando y lo duro
nos gusta masticar.

We like to eat chewy,
we like to eat smooth.

Nos gusta comer estando
sentados y también al andar.

We like to eat sitting
or while on the move.

Nos gusta comer juntos
y lento comemos.

We like eating together;
we like eating slow.

Nos gusta lo nuevo
y lo que ya conocemos.

We like to try new things
and foods that we know.

Nos gustan los colores ...

We like to eat colors ...

... que tiene la comida
y su forma y tamaño,
sea entera o partida.

... and all kinds of shapes.
We like eating whole foods
or slices and flakes.

Lo dulce nos gusta comer ...

We like to eat sweet ...

... y la "grasita" que es buena;
así nuestro cuerpo puede crecer
sano, ligero y fuerte.

... and "good fats" that are right
to help growing bodies stay both
strong and light.

Seguido y ligero nos gusta comer,
sea de mami o de una cuchara,
para pronto jugar y comer.

We like eating lightly, and often,
and soon, whether feeding from
mama or using our spoon.

La comida fría y caliente la comemos bien en la casa y también en la escuela.

We like to eat warm and we like to eat cool. We can eat well at home, we can eat well at school.

Lo que sea el alimento,
estemos afuera o adentro,
nos gusta comer bien
para estar sanos y esbeltos.

Whatever we eat, whether
outside or in, we like to eat well,
to be healthy and trim.

OTROS TÍTULOS DE INTERÉS DE LA EDITORIAL HOHM ~ SERIES DE SALUD PARA LA FAMILIA
OTHER TITLES FROM HOHM PRESS ~ FAMILY HEALTH SERIES

Nos Gusta Amamantar / We Like To Nurse
by Chia Martin
Illustrations by Shukyo Rainey

Español ISBN: 978-890772-41-3
papel, 32 páginas, $9,95

English ISBN: 978-934252-45-4,
paper, 32 pages, $9.95

Amamantar / Breastfeeding
by Regina Sara Ryan
and Deborah Auletta, CLE

Español ISBN: 978-1-890772-57-4
papel, 32 páginas, $9,95

English ISBN: 978-1-890772-48-2
paper, 32 pages, $9.95

Nos Gusta Vivir Verde / We Like To Live Green
by Mary Young

Español ISBN: 978-1-935387-01-5
papel, 32 páginas, $9,95

English ISBN: 978-1-935387-00-8
paper, 32 pages, $9.95

Nos Gusta Tocar Música / We Like To Play Music
by Kate Parker

Español ISBN: 978-1-890772-90-1
papel, 32 páginas, $9,95

English ISBN: 978-1-890772-85-7
paper, 32 pages, $9.95

PEDIDOS / ORDERS: 800-381-2700 • www.hohmpress.com

* Descuentos especiales por mayoreo. / Special discounts for bulk orders. *